SUPERBOOK®
ROAR!
DANIEL AND THE LIONS' DEN

Most Charisma House Book Group products are available at special quantity discounts for bulk purchase for sales promotions, premiums, fund-raising, and educational needs. For details, call us at (407) 333-0600 or visit our website at charismahouse.com.

Story adapted by Gwen Ellis and published by Charisma House, 600 Rinehart Road, Lake Mary, Florida 32746

An application to register this book for cataloging has been submitted to the Library of Congress.

International Standard Book Number: 978-1-62999-740-7

This publication is translated in Spanish under the title ¡Rugir! Daniel y el foso de los leones, copyright © 2020 by The Christian Broadcasting Network, Inc. CBN.com; published by Casa Creación, a Charisma Media company. All rights reserved.

20 21 22 23 24 — 987654321

Printed in China

It was a great day at the skateboard park. Chris skated through a tunnel and over a ramp, then spun up in the air to land right by his friend Joy and his robot, Gizmo.

"Oh yeah!" exclaimed Chris as he took off his helmet. "Just call me Sweet Air Feet!"

At that moment a big kid decided he wanted a younger boy's skateboard—and he took it.

"Give it back," the boy said.

"Make me," said the bully, and he skated away.

"Chris, you've got to do something," Joy said.

"Who, me?" replied Chris. "I don't even know them."

"Why does that matter?" Joy said. "You have to stand up when someone smaller is in trouble."

"So that bully can pound both of us?" Chris asked.

He wasn't sure what to do, so he didn't do anything at all. "Maybe we should go home," he said.

Suddenly Superbook appeared, whisking Chris, Joy, and Gizmo off on an adventure.

"I am taking you to meet a man who stood up for what he believed was right, even though it was the most dangerous choice," said Superbook.

And just like that, the three landed in a real palace with a real king.

Chris whispered, "Where are we, Giz?" The robot replied that they were in the ancient city of Babylon, about five hundred years before Jesus was born!

What kind of person would they meet who would choose to do right even when it was very hard?

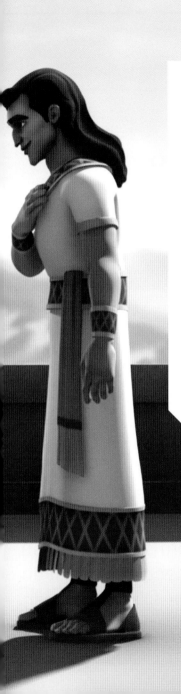

The children heard a man say, "You summoned me, King Darius?"

"Daniel, my friend!" said the king happily. "Thank you for everything you have done for my kingdom. You are always so wise."

Daniel replied, "My wisdom comes from God Almighty, who gives me strength as I pray to Him."

"Ah, Daniel, if I could just believe the way you believe in your God."

But then Chris, Joy, and Gizmo overheard some evil men talking. They were jealous of the king's friend! "We must do something about how the king favors Daniel," said one man.

Another moaned, "Yes, but we can't find any fault in his work!"

"Daniel prays three times a day to his God," the third man said. "I know a way we can use that to get rid of him!"

Chris gasped, "Those guys are out to get Daniel!"

"We have to help him," said Joy.

Those three evil men didn't waste any time. They made up a new law that decreed: "Listen, citizens of Babylon. For the next thirty days, anyone who prays to any god or man except the king shall be thrown into the lions' den." They wrote this

new rule on a scroll and brought it to King Darius. He didn't realize it was a trick to harm Daniel, so the king signed the law—which meant it could never be changed!

Oh my! That was awful! Chris, Joy, and Gizmo hurried as fast as they could to warn Daniel. Maybe he could hide or run away!

When they got to his house, they introduced themselves and said, "There is a plot to have you killed!"

Joy explained, "The king just issued a law declaring that if people pray to anyone except him, they'll be thrown into the lions' den!" Daniel immediately understood what that meant. He could die simply for praying to God!

Joy asked him, "What are you going to do?"

"What I always do when I am troubled," Daniel answered. "I pray." He opened the window and kneeled in prayer, thanking God and asking for His help—just as he always did.

Joy said, "I wish I had your strength."

Daniel explained that God wants people to share everything with Him— their needs, their questions, and their problems. Daniel knew that when people pray, God will answer! Joy bowed her head and closed her eyes.

"Maybe you should pray in secret," Chris suggested. He closed the window so no one could see Daniel praying.

But Daniel said, "Instead of fearing people, I must trust God. If I don't do what's right, I will have no strength at all." With that Daniel opened the window to pray—even though he knew the king could not save him if he kept praying to God.

It didn't take long for those evil men to come by and see what Daniel was doing.

"We are here to arrest you," they announced. "You're coming with us!" Soldiers grabbed Daniel and dragged him away to the palace.

There, the men told King Darius that they had caught Daniel praying to God and not to the king.

Uh-oh. That wasn't what the king wanted at all! Daniel was his good friend. He didn't want him to die! But he had signed the scroll, making it a law that couldn't be changed. Sadly, King Darius realized he could not help his friend.

He looked right at Daniel and said, "May your God rescue you."

The guards took Daniel away and threw him into a den of hungry lions! Next they put a huge stone over the opening so no one could rescue him.

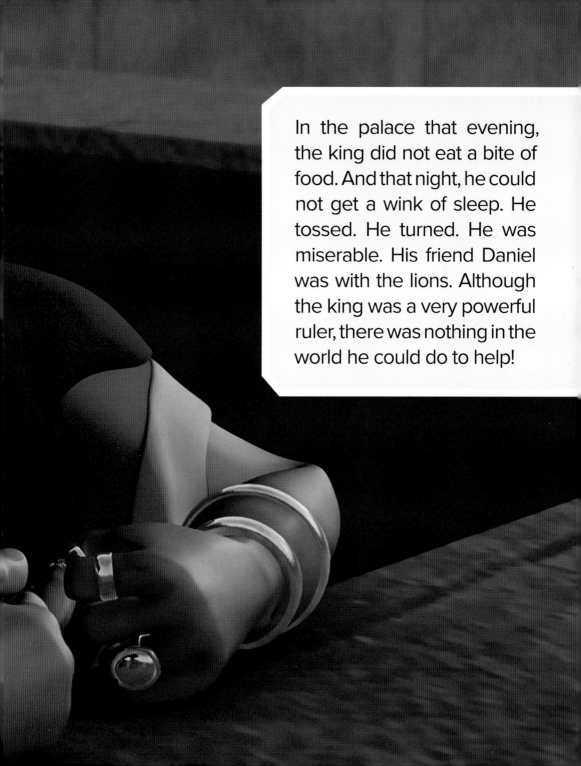

In the palace that evening, the king did not eat a bite of food. And that night, he could not get a wink of sleep. He tossed. He turned. He was miserable. His friend Daniel was with the lions. Although the king was a very powerful ruler, there was nothing in the world he could do to help!

King Darius could not wait for the sun to come up. Very early the next morning, he rushed to the lions' den to check on his friend.

"Move the stone," the king commanded.

Chris, Joy, and Gizmo watched as the guards slowly opened the pit. The king shouted loudly, "Daniel, servant of the living God! Was your God able to rescue you from the lions?"

Everyone waited nervously.

Finally, from deep down in the pit came a strong voice.

"Long live the king!" Daniel called. "My God sent His angel to shut the lions' mouths!"

When Daniel was lifted out of the pit, the king was thrilled to see that his friend wasn't even scratched!

King Darius then told his entire kingdom about Daniel's God, declaring: "He is the living God. He rescues and saves His people. He performs miracles and wonders, and He has rescued Daniel from the power of the lions."

Just then Superbook took Chris, Joy, and Gizmo back to the skate park. And guess what? That big bully was still picking on the smaller kid.

He sneered, "Come get your skateboard, you baby."

But something was different now. Well really, *someone* was different now. Chris was different. He said, "If Daniel could do the right thing, so can I." Then he walked right up to the bully and told him to give back the skateboard.

"Says who?" asked the bully.

"Says me," answered Chris firmly. Then Joy, Gizmo, the little boy, and the other kids in the park all said, "Me too!" The bully was outnumbered.

"Ah, who cares?" he mumbled, backing away. But he accidentally stepped on Gizmo's foot, hitting the switch for the robot's rocket!

Gizmo blasted off with the bully, and they went spiraling and swerving all over the skateboard park. It was a ride the boy would always remember—especially if he ever thought about bullying another kid again.

"The earnest prayer of a righteous person has great power and produces wonderful results."

—James 5:16